DATE DUE

DEC 4 '90			
FEB 25 '91			
OCT 18 '94			
OCT 26 1994			

TWO FRIENDS

GUY DE MAUPASSANT
Illustrations by
ETIENNE DELESSERT

CREATIVE EDUCATION

English Translation: Gerard Hopkins
Editor: Ann Redpath, Design: Rita Marshall
Biographical Sketch: Virginia Sheff

Published by Creative Education, Inc. 123 South
Broad Street, Mankato, Minnesota 56001

Printed in the United States.

Acknowledgement: the translation by Gerard Hopkins
was first published by the Folio Society.

Library of Congress Catalog Card No.: 85-71456
de Maupassant, Guy: Two Friends
Mankato, MN: Creative Education; 32 p.; ISBN: 0-88682-003-0

CREATIVE'S CLASSIC STORIES

This short story is taken out of an anthology and presented in its own volume where it stands a better chance of being read and remembered.

In one story, we might see a character survive extreme loneliness, danger, or sadness. Reading about such characters and events can be a powerful experience. And once we've read a good story, it can stay dormant in our memories for years and come to the surface later when we need its wisdom in facing our own danger, loneliness or sadness.

This short story is a well-told classic which has stood the test of time. It is included in Creative's Classic Stories Series and presented with all the dignity and richness a good classic story deserves.

PARIS WAS SURROUNDED, STARVING, AT its last gasp. There were fewer and fewer sparrows on the roofs. The sewers had been emptied of their population. People were eating anything they could find.

One bright January morning, as Monsieur Morissot, a watchmaker by profession, and a man who loved to take his ease when occasion offered, was strolling in a melancholy mood along the outer boulevard, with his hands in the pockets of his army trousers and a void in his stomach, he ran into a man whom he immediately recognized. It was Monsieur Sauvage, a riverside acquaintance.

Every Sunday morning before the war, Monsieur Morissot had been in the habit of setting off early, with a bamboo rod in his hand and a tin box slung on his back. He took the Argenteuil train, got out at Colombes, and walked to the small island which goes by the name of Marante. As soon as he reached this place of his dreams, he settled down to fish, and he fished till nightfall.

A tubby, jovial little man was always there before him, a draper from the Rue Notre-Dame-de-Lorette, as fanatical an angler as himself. They frequently spent half the day sitting side-by-side, rod in hand, and their feet dangling over the stream. They had become fast friends.

Sometimes they did not talk at all. Sometimes they chatted, but so alike were their tastes and their reactions, and so perfect their understanding of each other, that words were unnecessary.

Sometimes, on spring mornings, about ten o'clock, when the early sun had laid on the still surface of the river a faint mist, which flowed with the current, and beat down on the backs of the two enthusiasts with the welcome warmth of the waxing season, Morissot would say to his neighbor, "Lovely, isn't it?" And Monsieur Sauvage would reply, "I don't know anything lovelier." That simple exchange was enough to bring complete understanding between them, and make them like one another the more.

On autumn afternoons, when the day was nearing its end and the setting sun reddened the sky, when the water reflected crimson clouds and the far horizon seemed all ablaze, when the figures of the two friends seemed lit by fire, and the trees, already turning red, glowed and shivered with a foretaste of winter. Monsieur Sauvage would smile at Morissot and say: "That's a sight for sore eyes." And Morissot, struck with the wonder of it all, but keeping his eyes firmly fixed on his float, would answer: "Better than the boulevard, eh?"

No sooner had the two friends recognized each other, than they shook hands warmly, caught up in a little eddy of emotion at meeting thus again in such different circumstances. Monsieur Sauvage sighed and said: "What times we live in!" And Morissot, all gloom, lamented: "And what a lovely day! The first really good weather of the year!"

That was undeniable, for the sky was an unclouded, brilliant blue.

They walked together, side-by-side, thoughtful and sad.

"Remember our fishing?" said Morissot. "Those were the days."

"Will they ever come again, I wonder?" said Monsieur Sauvage.

They went into a little café and had an absinthe each. Then they resumed their walk along the pavement.

Suddenly Morissot pulled up short: "What about another?" "I'm with you," said Monsieur Sauvage, and they turned in at the second bar. By the time they left it they were slightly fuddled, as men are apt to be after drinking spirits on an empty stomach. The day was mild, and a pleasant breeze fanned their faces.

Monsieur Sauvage had been made more than a little drunk by the air. He stopped and put a question:

"Why shouldn't we have a shot?"

"What at?"

"Fishing."

"Where?"

"At our island, of course. The French outposts are close to Colombes. I know the colonel in command—a chap called Dumoulin. He won't make any difficulties."

Quivering with anticipation Morissot acquiesced: "Done. I'm with you." And the two friends separated to get their equipment.

An hour later they were striding together down the main road. They reached the villa in which the colonel had established his headquarters. He smiled at their odd request, but readily gave his consent. They started off again, armed with the necessary permit.

In next to no time they had crossed the outpost line, passed through Colombes which had been evacuated, and found themselves on the edge of a small vineyard which sloped down to the Seine. It was about eleven o'clock.

Opposite them the village of Argenteuil seemed dead. The heights of Orgemont and Sannois dominated the countryside. The great plain which stretches as far as Nanterre was empty, completely empty, with its leafless cherry trees and gray soil.

Monsieur Sauvage pointed with his finger at the high ground "The Prussians are up there," he said. A sort of paralysis seized upon the two friends as they gazed at the desert before them.

The Prussians! They had never set eyes on them, but for months and months they had been conscious of their presence on every side, bringing ruin on France, looting, murdering, spreading starvation, invisible, irresistable. A sort of superstitious dread was added to the hate they felt for that unknown and victorious race.

Hesitant and fearful, Morissot said: "Suppose we met some of them?"

In spite of everything, the mocking note of the Paris streets sounded in his friend's reply: "We would offer them a fish fry!"

But they still hesitated before venturing out into the open country, for they were intimidated by the vast spread of silence round them.

It was Monsieur Sauvage who finally took the plunge.

"We'd better get going," he said, "but keep your weather eye open!"

They clambered down through the vines, bent double, crawling on hands and knees, taking advantage of the cover offered by the bushes, their ears pricked.

They still had a strip of open ground to cross before they could get to the river bank. They broke into a run, and, when they reached it, went to the earth in a thicket of dry reeds.

Morissot put his ear to the ground to catch the sound of footsteps. He heard nothing.

They were alone.

Plucking up their courage, they began to fish.

Immediately in front, the deserted island of Marante hid them from the other bank. The little restaurant was closed, and looked as though it had been abandoned for years.

Monsieur Sauvage caught the first gudgeon, Morissot the second, and then, with scarcely a pause, they kept jerking up their rods with little silver creatures flickering at the end of their lines. A miraculous draught of fish, indeed!

Carefully, they put their haul into a fine-meshed net dangling in the water at their feet, and a delicious joy took hold of them, a joy that comes when a favorite pleasure is resumed after long months of deprivation.

The kindly sun sent a ripple of warmth between their shoulder blades. There was not a sound to be heard, nor was there a thought in their heads. The world was forgotten. They were fishing.

But, suddenly, a dull, a seemingly subterranean sound made the earth tremble. The big guns were at it again.

Morissot turned his head, and above the bank, away to the left, he saw the great bulk of Mont Valérien with, on its head, a white plume, a drift of smoke which it had just spewed out.

Almost immediately a second jet of smoke leaped from the summit of the fort, and a few moments later the noise of a second detonation reached their ears.

Others followed, and at brief intervals the mount puffed out its death-dealing breath, spreading clouds of milky vapor which slowly rose into the peaceful sky, covering it with a pall.

Monsieur Sauvage shrugged. "There they are, at it again," he said.

Morissot, who was anxiously watching the little feather on his float bobbing up and down, was suddenly filled with the anger of a man of peace at the maniacs with no thought for anything but fighting. "Only fools," he grunted, "would go on killing each other like that!"

"They're worse than fools," said Monsieur Sauvage.

Morissot, who had just landed a fish, burst out with: "Nothing'll ever change so long as there are governments!"

Monsieur Sauvage corrected him: "A republic would never have declared war . . ."

But Morissot cut him short: "With kings there are foreign wars; with republics, civil strife."

Without heat they started arguing the great political issues, showing all the sweet reasonableness of peace-loving men who cannot see beyond their noses. On one thing only they agreed: that mankind would never be free. And all the while Mont Valérien kept thundering, bringing destruction on French homes, grinding flesh and blood to dust, crushing human bodies, and bringing to the hearts of women, girls, and mothers in other lands an endless suffering.

"Such is life," said Monsieur Sauvage.

"Say, rather, such is death," laughed Morissot.

They both gave a frightened start. They had a feeling that somebody was moving behind them. Turning their heads they saw, standing at their backs, four great hulking brutes, armed and bearded, dressed like liveried footmen, with flat caps on their heads, and rifles leveled.

The rods dropped from their hands and went floating down the river.

In a matter of seconds they were seized, carried off, flung into a boat, and ferried across to the island.

Behind the building they had thought deserted, they saw about twenty German soldiers.

A sort of hairy giant astride upon a chair and smoking a long porcelain pipe, asked them in excellent French: "Did you have good fishing, gentlemen?"

One of the soldiers laid the net filled with fish at the officer's feet. The Prussian smiled:

"Not too bad, I see. But we have other things to think about. Just listen to me and don't worry.

"So far as I am concerned you are two spies sent to keep watch on me. I have taken you and I shall shoot you. You have been pretending to fish, the better to conceal your real intentions. You have fallen into my hands. So much the worse for you: but war is war.

"Since, however, you came through your own lines, I take it that you have been given the countersign which will enable you to return the same way. Give that countersign to me and I will spare your lives."

The two friends stood side-by-side with ashen faces. Their hands were twitching nervously, but they said nothing.

The officer went on: "No one will be the wiser. You will return undisturbed. The secret will go with you. If you refuse, you die—instantly. Which will you choose?"

They still stood motionless. Not a word came from them.

Quite calmly, the Prussian pointed to the river, and continued: "In five minutes you will be at the bottom of that. Five minutes. I suppose you have relatives?"

Mont Valérien was still thundering.

The two fisherman stood perfectly still and silent. The German gave an order in his own language. Then he moved his chair so as not to be too close to the prisoners, and twelve men marched up and halted at a distance of twenty paces, their rifles at the order.

"I give you one minute now, not a second more."

Then he got quickly to his feet, approached the two Frenchmen, took Morissot by the arm, and led him to one side. In a low voice, he said: "Give me the countersign. Your friend need know nothing. I will make it look as though I have relented."

Morissot said nothing.

The Prussian repeated the maneuver with Monsieur Sauvage, and made the same suggestion to him.

Monsieur Sauvage said nothing.

They were back as they had been,

side-by side.

The officer gave an order. The soldiers raised their rifles.

Morissot's eyes happened to fall on the netful of gudgeon lying in the grass quite close to him.

A ray of sunshine fell on the pile of still-squirming fish, and made them glitter. He was guilty of a moment's weakness. In spite of his effort to hold them back, two tears came into his eyes.

"Good-by, Monsieur Sauvage," he said unsteadily.

"Good-by, Monsieur Morissot," Monsieur Sauvage said.

They shook hands, trembling

uncontrollably from head to foot.

"Fire!" shouted the officer.

The twelve shots rang out like one.

Monsieur Sauvage fell forward like a log. Morissot, who was taller, swayed, spun round, and collapsed across his friend. He lay with his face to the sky, a few drops of blood bubbling from holes in the front of his coat.

The German issued some further orders. His men scattered and came back with some lengths of rope and a few stones which they fastened to the feet of the dead men. Then they carried them to the bank.

Mont Valérien was still thundering. By this time there was a great mountain of smoke above it.

Two soldiers lifted Morissot by the head and feet. Two others did the same with Monsieur Sauvage. The bodies were swung violently backwards and forwards for a few moments, then pitched into the river, where they fell feet foremost, the stones weighing them down.

The water splashed, seethed, quivered, then grew calm again. A few small ripples broke against the bank.

A little blood floated on the surface.

The officer, still entirely unperturbed, said, in a low voice: "It is the fishes' turn now."

He noticed the net of gudgeon on the grass.

He picked it up, looked it over, smiled and called: "Wilhelm!"

A soldier in a white apron hurried up.

The officer threw him the haul of the two shot fisherman, and said:

"Fry these little creatures, quickly, while they are still alive. They will be delicious."

Then, he returned to his pipe.

GUY DE MAUPASSANT

Guy de Maupassant was a French realist writer, who observed and reported on the world with detachment. While he wrote with some sympathy for common people, his stories generally reflected a gloomy and ironic outlook on life.

Maupassant was born on August 5, 1850, in the Normandy region of France and was educated there. He spent a year of service in the Franco-Prussian War after which he earned a living as a government clerk and later as a literary journalist. During this time, he studied to become a writer.

A conscientious and exacting craftsman, Maupassant had studied diligently under the guidance of his godfather, novelist Gustave

Flaubert. After ten years, Maupassant considered himself master of the writer's craft and destroyed all his previous work. In the next ten years, he wrote sixteen volumes of short stories, three collections of travel sketches, six novels, and a volume of verse.

At Maupassant's graveside, another great French writer, Emile Zola told mourners that their friend had been one of the happiest of men and one of the unhappiest. Maupassant was a great joker who delighted in telling boastful lies about himself. He spent the money his literary achievement brought him extravagantly—he enjoyed the sporting life in the country and a dissolute life in the city.

Maupassant's suffering was from continual

overwork, intense headaches, and syphilis. He died in a Paris asylum on July 6, 1893, raving mad.